Akea

His Mother's Son

Book two in the Akea series

Elizabeth Jade

To learn more about this author, please visit:
www.elizabethjade.org

Other books in the *Akea* Series

Book 1: Akea – The Power of Destiny

The beautiful illustrations in this book are all by Anthony Wallis.

Pronunciation Guide

Akea	ah-key-uh
Kazakh	kah-zac
Gwenevier	gwen-er-veer
Adair	uh-dare
Salvador	sal-vuh-door
Raghnal	rag-nul
Maska	mass-kah
Javier	jay-vee-er
Hailie	hay-lee
Fantine	fan-teen
Rakin	rack-in
Bluinse	blue-in-zee

ISBN: 978-1-9162285-9-7

Published by

i2i
PUBLISHING

i2i Publishing. Manchester.

www.i2ipublishing.co.uk

CHAPTER 1

A great snowfall had held the vast and pleasant land within its wintery grip for what seemed like a lifetime. Now, at long last, spring had taken its place in the great circle of seasons. The sun passed slowly over the pack's mountain home, sharing its much-needed warmth, and small clusters of flowers lay nestled in patches of sunlight, their purple heads nodding gently in the passing breeze. A silvery-grey muzzle sniffed a group of sweet-scented blooms before gazing out at the land beneath him. It was his duty as alpha male to patrol the wolf pack's territory each day and he took this responsibility seriously, even though it was not always easy.

Ambling playfully behind him were his three-month-old pups, four gorgeous bundles of fun, eager to discover this exciting new world. Kazakh had named his pups with care, studying their looks and personalities as his father had done before him, and as they trotted past him, he smiled thoughtfully.

First in line was Gwenevier, meaning 'white wave'- a perfect choice with her white wavy coat. Then her sister, Fayth, named in memory of his own mate's beloved sister. This little one was quiet and thoughtful, like her namesake. She had odd-coloured eyes with thick black rings around them which stood out against her red-tinged coat. The third pup was Adair, a large bold male who looked more like his mother. And finally...

"Wait! Stop!" he cried, and the three pups stopped in a neat straight line. They could sense that something was wrong. Kazakh stooped as he counted them - *one, two, three... four?* No, there were only three. "Who's missing?" he asked anxiously. Kazakh inspected each one in turn, repeating their names as he went. "Gwenevier, Fayth, Adair... Salvador." he muttered crossly. It was always Salvador.

On the edge of a rocky outcrop some distance away, sat Salvador. He was taller and more wolf-like in appearance than his siblings. Even from a distance, it was easy to see the others were not pure wolf, but not Salvador, he was every inch a wolf pup. Nevertheless, despite having inherited his father's looks, this fine young male was far more like his husky mother, Akea, in behaviour. He always sat away from his littermates, looking out into the distance as if he were searching for something, but didn't quite understand what it was.

Salvador was so deep in thought that he had failed to notice his father approaching. Kazakh nudged him to one side and sat down in his place. Salvador glanced briefly at his siblings who were playing happily behind them, then hung his head submissively. He could tell he was in trouble again. An awkward silence followed as Kazakh searched for the right words to discipline his son.

"Now then my son," he began, in a voice that was stern yet kind. "This is not the first time you have disobeyed me by wandering off, nor do I think it shall be the last. What do I tell you and your brother and sisters?" Salvador turned to his father with a milky-eyed look that was sure to soften the hardest of hearts.

"To stay close to you, so we don't get lost or killed," he whispered.

"Well at least you have been listening to my words, even if you do not always put them to good use," commended Kazakh.

Kazakh called to his pups and together they set off towards their cave. This time he made sure Salvador was right beside him, though now and then he looked back to check his other pups were still following obediently. When they approached the safety of the alpha's cave, the pack members bowed low in greeting. Kazakh left the pups in their care and went into the cave to greet his mate, Akea, with the affectionate licking and nuzzling required.

"That son of ours," he sighed, lying down and resting his chin on his tired paws. "He wandered off again. I don't know what to do with him." Akea rolled her eyes and shook her head in mock annoyance.

"Honestly, that pup," she said. "He's so... so..."

"Like his mother?" he teased. "And look at the trouble she got into."

Akea leapt onto Kazakh, knocking him to the ground and the two of them tussled playfully for a while. The game was a welcome distraction, but it could not stop Kazakh from being concerned. Although a husky, Akea was a descendant of the legendary Great White Wolf, and even when very young, Kazakh had sensed there was something different about her. There was something different about Salvador too, and it made him nervous. In her short time as Queen, Akea had become the most loved and respected of leaders, but her path there had been a difficult one and it had made him rather overprotective of his offspring.

A distinctive howl rang through the air and they wandered out of the cave to investigate. Akea surveyed her pack with its husky sentry standing erect.

"Is something amiss, Raghnal?" she called down.

"No, your majesty, but it is almost time to hunt. What are your instructions?"

"Very well," she said. "Follow me."

Akea descended the rocks gracefully and the pack bowed before following her down into the forest. Kazakh had decided some time ago that he and several others would remain behind to guard the cave and the pups during a hunt. It allowed him to keep a close eye on Salvador, who at this point was slouching moodily by his sleeping littermates. His mother and the rest of the pack marched into the shimmering distance, looking like a formidable army. They soon tracked down the musk deer, thanks to their excellent sense of smell.

"Look! Over there!" whispered Raghnal, his head lowered, ready for stalking. He watched Akea carefully, awaiting her orders.

Akea's blue eyes scanned the unsuspecting herd, looking for the best positions for attack. Then she closed them, focusing her mind on the task ahead. After a while, she opened her eyes and nodded. The pack obediently fanned out and began their approach.

CHAPTER 2

Kazakh stood on top of a high flat rock, surveying the vast green land that made up his pack's territory. In his father's time, the pack had lived down in the forest and only the Wolf Queen had lived in the mountains. Now his pack's alpha female *was* the Wolf Queen, and even Akea with all her talents, could not live in two places at once. The sound of falling stones caught his attention, and he turned to find Fayth climbing up toward him.

"Hello Father, may I sit with you please?" she asked quietly. Kazakh nodded and his daughter sat neatly beside him as he returned to his sentry duty. Her unusual eyes gave her a fierce look, but she was really a docile and thoughtful pup.

"What are the others doing?" he asked, leaning over briefly to lick his little one.

"Oh, they're asleep."

"Goodness, even Salvador?"

"Yes, even him," she replied with a smile, head tilted, and one eyebrow raised in such a way that he couldn't stop himself from smiling too.

The two wolves sat quietly side by side, staring out into the distance with the breeze gently brushing their shaggy coats. They sat this way for some time before Fayth spoke again.

"I wonder if our homeland will be full of peace and happiness forever or if something will change it," she muttered to herself. "Trouble is bound to come one day; it always does in the end. I hope we will be ready for it."

Kazakh gave his daughter a quizzical sideways glance. He was both surprised and alarmed by her words. Akea's sister had been known for making profound statements, and it was rather worrying to hear his own daughter doing the same.

Just then, Kazakh heard the grumbling of hungry wolves and he carried Fayth down to ground level, gently placing her in the patchy grass before speaking to the remaining pack members.

"Do not complain so. The Queen will return soon, and we shall all eat our fill."

Kazakh's brother, Maska, pushed his way to the front where he stood looking at him intently, his posture far from submissive. He was taller than Kazakh, even though he was younger, and his quarrelsome personality was in a class all of its own. He stared menacingly at him with his tail erect; his brown eyes half hidden by his shaggy coat.

"We should find something for ourselves," he insisted. "A strong pack such as ours should allow no one to be kept hungry."

Kazakh sighed deeply. When he and his brother were children, their games had always been battles for dominance, and their poor father had a hard time keeping them apart. Things hadn't really changed much, for whenever Maska spoke you could tell he was looking for trouble.

"It is not your decision to make, my brother. Unless of course you would like to come up here and take my place as alpha male. Or maybe you would prefer to wait for the pack's return and take your point up with the Queen," he replied in a threatening tone.

For a moment, Kazakh appeared to have the upper hand and Maska knew he'd been outmanoeuvred, but he couldn't back down without one final statement.

"Well, I wouldn't mind," he muttered as he turned to leave. "After all, Akea's only a husky. What chance would she have against a proper volk like me?"

There was a loud thud as Kazakh knocked him to the ground, crushing the grass beneath. The other wolves jumped back in alarm. Some whined, nervously licking their lips, while others edged forward, hackles raised, unsure who to attack and who to defend.

"You hold your tongue, or I shall be forced to remove it," snarled Kazakh breathlessly. Maska struggled beneath him and it took all of Kazakh's strength to keep him pinned there.

"You wouldn't have the nerve," gasped Maska.

Kazakh knew his brother was right. The ties of flesh and blood were stronger than his temper, but in front of the remaining wolves, he could not allow Maska's treacherous words to go unpunished. He had no choice but to act.

"In truth, I should kill you, but out of respect for our father I am prepared to offer you banishment instead of death. Is that generous enough for you?"

Maska nodded and Kazakh allowed him to get up. The other wolves had formed a protective half circle behind Kazakh. One wolf tried to prove his own loyalty by licking

Kazakh's muzzle, but in a fit of temper Kazakh snapped at him and the youngster rolled submissively onto his side. Maska had been about to speak, but decided discretion would be the wiser course, and with a barely noticeable bow, he turned and trotted into the distance.

A moment later, Akea and her group returned to the pack with the remains of not one, but two deer carcasses, and both the pups and the remaining wolves began to feed. However, Akea sensed all was not well. Kazakh seemed rather tense and a little out of breath.

"Well, what's wrong?" she asked quietly. Her mate was typically reluctant to answer and wandered into the cave, leaving Akea to follow.

"Well?" she repeated, and Kazakh fidgeted a little - communication had never been his strong point.

"Maska was making trouble again. His words and actions were treasonable, and I had no choice but to banish him."

"Oh, I see. Well, I would probably have done the same, but remember what happened with your sister and be on your guard," she replied, licking him reassuringly about the muzzle.

They rejoined the pack unnoticed, and all ate happily as the sun sank below the horizon. The earlier confrontation still troubled Kazakh, and Akea's warning about his sister made him question his decision to banish Maska. He had once fought with his sister, Bluinse, over Akea's selection as Wolf Queen, and she had managed to turn the whole pack against Akea for a while. He desperately hoped that this time, he would not be proved wrong.

Come nightfall, they were all fast asleep, with Raghnal and Javier as sentries; all that is except for Salvador. He lay in the entrance to the alpha's cave with his family sleeping soundly behind him. He felt restless. Like his mother before him, he longed for something that he could feel but was unable to describe. His siblings would not understand and would probably tease him, except perhaps for Fayth - she had inherited her mother's gentleness and wisdom. Salvador sighed; he was convinced his destiny lay beyond the wolf pack and not even his over-protective father would be able to stop it.

CHAPTER 3

The days passed without disturbance, and in time, the seasons themselves turned full circle. There had been no sign of Maska, despite Akea's concern, and Kazakh began to think he would not be troubling them again after all.

In the peaceful night sky, the full moon shone down on the sleeping pack. Fayth's rich, red coat glistened in the moonlight. With a white blaze on her forehead and white tips to her paws and tail, she looked just like a husky. Her looks made her easy to find among the sleeping wolves.

It was easy to find Salvador too, but for quite a different reason. Each night he lay alone at the edge of the wolf pack, staring out into the darkness. He had grown into a fine young wolf, his thick black coat hiding his only husky features, his serious looking amber eyes. Salvador pawed at the side of his muzzle before tucking up his feet and rolling onto his back. He gazed up at the sparkling sky, listening to the sounds of the nocturnal animals.

"May I join you?" came a voice from behind. Salvador twisted over and saw Javier standing nearby, twitching his tail. He nodded and Javier strode over, head lowered submissively. Javier licked him briefly and lay down beside him.

"What are you thinking?" he asked, and Salvador sighed deeply.

"You wouldn't understand, Javier."

"A friend doesn't always need to understand, they just need to listen," he answered, and Salvador smiled. His mother always liked Javier and he could see why.

"To be honest, I don't quite understand it myself. All I know is that I feel different." Javier thought for a moment.

"I am sure it will pass, Salvador. After all, your mother felt the same when she first joined the pack, and the only real difference between you and your mother is that being born in the wild, you have never met a human and she has."

"And I never will either," replied Salvador in a curious fashion that made Javier look at him warily.

"You shouldn't say such things," he whispered.

"Why not? It's true."

"Because humans are unpredictable creatures; some are good and some are bad, and you will never know which until it is too late. Why not ask your mother? No one knows the truth of this more than she does."

Nervously, Javier stood up, licked Salvador's muzzle and walked away, keeping his tail lowered in submission. In the old wolf pack, Javier had been an omega. These wolves only had scraps of food to eat and were on the receiving end of everyone else's bad tempers. When Akea and Kazakh took over, they declared all wolves below the alpha pair to be equal. Such submissive behaviour was now unnecessary, but somehow Javier couldn't get out of the habit.

Salvador returned to his star gazing. Javier meant well, but how could someone who was so much a part of the pack, truly understand how it felt 'not to belong'.

Suddenly, a strange rattling sound came out of the darkness and the pack woke with a start. All eyes were on their Queen, who stood with her hackles raised and her ears pricked. Sensing her concern, Kazakh moved to stand beside her.

"What's wrong, what is that noise?" he asked. Akea's blue eyes were wide with alarm as she scanned the darkness.

"That is the sound of a vehicle," she replied anxiously, "The sound of humans."

"That's not possible," insisted Kazakh. "They have never come this close before and besides, what would they be doing all the way out here in the middle of the night?"

"I don't know why they are here Kazakh, but they are. Something is wrong, very wrong indeed," she whispered as the sound vanished, replaced by an eerie silence. The pack was equally silent. No one moved. All eyes were fixed on Akea who stood listening intently.

A gun blast burst through the silence, scattering the pack in blind panic. There were wolves running in all directions, caught for brief moments in the glare of the humans' torchlights as they burst through the trees. It was utter chaos, and for the first time in her reign, Akea felt out of control.

The night air filled with the sound of wolves yapping and people shouting, followed by a blood-curdling cry that made Akea turn and head quickly down towards a Land Rover. Her maternal instincts told her that one of her own offspring was in serious trouble.

"Over here," came a voice. "I've got one."

Curled up in a capture net and pinned down by the neck and rump, lay Salvador. The other men gathered around to examine their catch. Just as Akea reached the vehicle, Kazakh appeared. He snarled and snapped at the men, desperately trying to reach his son. After all he had done to protect his children, he was not about to let the humans take one from him now.

One man reached for his gun, but Akea had almost lost Kazakh to a gunshot wound before and she was not about to let it happen again. Without fear, she sank her teeth into the man's arm, causing him to drop the gun and stagger back, as much in surprise at the aggression from this mysterious husky as in the pain from his injury. The sight of his parents broke through his fear and Salvador thrashed about, ears flat and teeth bared.

Then came a sharp pain in his shoulder, followed by a spinning sensation. He staggered for a moment, his legs no longer working together before collapsing unconscious. Akea joined Kazakh as another man fired a shot just over their heads, forcing them to retreat. Akea was heartbroken, but there was nothing they could do to help Salvador now. She had no choice but to leave him behind. Akea closed her eyes for a moment, wishing him well with all her heart, and then she and Kazakh turned and fled.

They spent the rest of the night curled up together in a small cave just beyond the border of their territory. It had been a terrifying time and Akea had no idea where the other pack members had taken shelter or if Salvador was the only one who was missing.

She and Kazakh made their way to the edge of their territory, just as the sun came up. Together they howled a low-pitched resonating howl, designed to reach into the distance. Their aim was to gather the pack together but howling on the edge of the territory like this could attract a rival pack who would be sure to attack them. Their howls were soon answered, and as their numbers grew, so did their safety.

They made their way through the territory, collecting more pack members as they went, and by the time they reached the Queen's cave, it was heart-wrenchingly clear that the only one missing was Salvador.

Chapter 4

The Land Rover bumped along the forest tracks, rocking its precious cargo back and forth. Salvador had been sleeping peacefully inside the travel crate, but as the vehicle reached the edge of the wood, the tranquilliser began to wear off and he started whimpering. He had been dreaming he was curled up outside the alpha's cave with his family, when suddenly there were gun shots, doors slamming and people shouting all around him. The vehicle bounced through a deep rut in the road, waking the youngster from his nightmare.

He tried to stand up, but the crate was too small, and he banged his head. Salvador lay down again, and as he glanced about, he realised he had not been dreaming after all. Full of questions, he tried to talk to the humans, but they could only hear barks and whimpers. Irritated by the noise, one man yelled at him to *shut up*, brandishing a gun to make his point, while the other just casually glanced at him before turning the radio on. With a heavy heart, Salvador realised that Javier was right; humans were extremely unpredictable creatures.

Eventually, the vehicle pulled up by a cabin near a row of enclosures and the rear door opened. At last, Salvador could see and smell the outside world and he didn't like what either sense presented him with. The strange men lifted his crate onto a trolley and pushed it across to the entrance of one of the enclosures. They slid the door open, but Salvador didn't move - there was a strange clinical smell which disturbed him. A sudden loud noise from behind sent him rushing for the only cover he could find - a wooden den on the far side. As he peered out on a concrete world dusted with hay, the men removed the crate and walked away, leaving an eerie silence behind them. It was then that the full impact of his situation dawned on him and Salvador threw himself to the floor, crying bitterly. Just then, a voice from nowhere brought an abrupt end to his crying fit.

"Salvador! Salvador!" The young wolf jumped to his feet and lowered his head. He began vigorously sniffing around the enclosure, trying to find the creature speaking to him.

"Who's there?" he called nervously, "Who are you? Where are you?"

"Salvador, it's me." The voice was soothing and familiar, and as he began to calm down, he realised it wasn't coming from within the enclosure, but from inside his head.

"Mother? Mother, is that really you? Where are you? Did they take you too?" As he spoke, he gadded about excitedly.

"Salvador, calm down this minute," snapped Akea, who at this point was standing alone on a rock above the Queen's cave. "They have not taken me. Sit down. You must restrain your emotions for I cannot keep this up for long." Salvador obediently did as she asked him but was still extremely puzzled.

"Why did they take me, Mother?" he asked.

"I cannot answer that, my dearest. All I can tell you is that I am certain you will return to us one day."

"But how?"

"You will be shown the way. You must be brave, and you must be strong. Remember, you are my son and a descendent of the Great Volk. If you believe in yourself, the way forward will be revealed to you. Everyone will come to know who you are."

"Will you speak to me again soon?"

"No, my son, for I must return to my duties. I sense troubled times ahead and I must prepare myself and the pack for whatever the future will bring."

"I wish I understood you, Mother."

"My beautiful boy," sighed Akea. "You will one day, and on that day, you will make us all proud. Goodbye my son, and may the Great Volk be with you."

The voice faded from his mind, leaving him just as confused as before. He had never understood when his mother spoke of such things, but she had promised that the Great Wolf would watch over him, and this knowledge gave him peace. He lay down with his head on his front paws and as he drifted into sleep, he whispered into his own mind:

"I love you!"

****

Akea smiled as she caught the faint words from Salvador. He had taken the first steps along his unique journey, but she was not about to leave him to face it alone. Akea raised her head and stared out into the distance, beyond the mountains and forests fading into the night. She was about to try something that, to her knowledge, had never been tried before, not even by a Wolf Queen: she would try to contact The Great Wolf himself, in what can only be described as 'Akea's Prayer'.

"Oh, Great One," she began, focusing her thoughts. "It is I, Akea – Tinnet's successor as Volk Queen... although I suppose you already know that. Indeed, it may well have been your doing. I beg you to watch over my son, Salvador, who was taken from me by the humans. See he journeys safely along the path that has been chosen for him, for I cannot help him now. This is a time of immense upheaval, and I must prepare myself and my pack for what may lie ahead. Oh, Great Volk, I believe that you exist. I have felt your influence in my own life. Help me now, I beg you."

A lump came up in Akea's throat as she held back the tears. She sensed the approach of the pack behind her but did not look back. Instead, she raised her head to the full moon nestled in the now dark and starry sky, and let out a long, mournful howl. It resonated clearly in the stillness of the night, and as its echo began to fade, she howled again. This time, Kazakh's rich, but equally sad tone joined hers as he came and sat beside her. Then, one by one, the other wolves joined the call until the sound of their howling could be heard for miles.

Fayth was the first to stop. Turning to her sister, Gwenevier, for comfort, Fayth buried her head in her sister's fur and wept. She loved her lost brother more than anyone and wished she could bring him back somehow. The howling faded into silence and the wolves returned to their caves, but as Akea turned to leave, she saw a large white wolf standing on a nearby outcrop. She stared at the figure for a moment, taking in the thick black stripe that ran from the beginning of his muzzle to the tip of his tail. He seemed strangely familiar, but before she could utter a word to Kazakh, the stranger had gone.

Chapter 5

Over the months that followed, Salvador grew accustomed to his new home at the wildlife park, but it had not been easy for him. Each morning he woke in his artificial cave, climbed up his artificial rock and lay by his artificial pool. His only consolation was that the water was real. He still wished he was back with his family, but his keeper, Max, was a kind man who spent a lot of time trying to make him happy, and Salvador had grown fond of him.

One morning, Salvador was playing lazily with a large plastic ball when he heard someone calling him.

"Sooty!"

Salvador cringed - he disliked the name so much that he would gladly have bitten the person responsible for it, had it not been Max. It hadn't taken the young man long to realise Salvador was part husky (even if he had kept it to himself), and he seemed to have a way with animals that Salvador found irresistible. He watched his friend approach with a wheelbarrow full of meat. Feeding time at the park was dull, but at least it was guaranteed. Salvador trotted over to the mesh door of his enclosure, wagging his tail gently in greeting, and Max tossed in the portions of a deer carcass.

"I've got a treat for you later, boy," he called cheerfully before walking away, leaving Salvador feeling rather sad. Even after all this time, he still felt strange eating alone. Solitude was not usual among wolves and he would close his eyes as he ate, imagining there were other wolves eating alongside him.

Early that afternoon, as Salvador lay in the entrance to his cave, he noticed some movement inside the previously empty enclosure beside his own. There had been some human activity a short time before, and although he was sure they had all gone, there was most certainly something moving in there now. It was all very strange.

He watched for a moment, unsure what to make of it, but he soon allowed curiosity to overcome caution and made his way over to the mesh, pressing his nose up against it and taking in a deep breath through his nostrils.

Suddenly, something threw itself against the mesh with such a ferocious snarling and snapping that Salvador leapt back in alarm. The vicious creature turned out to be no more than a young female wolf who was just as frightened and confused as he had been when he first arrived. He studied her for a moment, taking in her sable tan coat and walnut eyes before cautiously approaching the fence again, desperate to befriend the only wolf he had seen in months.

"It's alright," he said gently, making certain his posture matched his tone. "You are quite safe. My name is Salvador, who are you?" The other wolf continued to snarl at him, hackles raised, and lips curled. "Nice name," he replied, in a voice rich with sarcasm, "And you're very pretty too."

Puzzled by his strange response, the female stopped snarling and stared at him. Immediately her face softened, and although her ears remained pricked, she was more uncertain now than aggressive.

"Who are you and from where do you come?" she asked in a superior manner. Salvador thought for a moment - he had already given her his name and yet she was asking who he was. Then he understood: in the absence of the traditional exchange of information through sniffing, this young female had adopted a more formal approach.

"I am Salvador, son of Akea, the husky who rules as Volk Queen and son of Kazakh, the alpha male who succeeded his father, Leopardo. I was taken from my mountain homeland during a night raid by the humans. Tell me please: who are you and from where do you come?"

She stared at him as he stood there expectantly. Then with one word, she turned her back on him and walked away with her head and tail held high. She left poor Salvador sad and hurt, with the word 'mongrel' ringing in his ears. Her harsh words made him aware, for the first time, that not everyone approved of his mother's role as Queen, even though the former Wolf Queen herself had given her blessing.

Salvador sighed deeply. He missed his mother more than he cared to admit, but as he turned to walk away, he stopped. He may be a 'mongrel' as she put it, but he was not about to let her think he was ashamed of his background. His mother was a descendant of the Great Wolf himself, and if that was good enough for the old Queen then it was good enough for him.

"Now look here!" he yelled angrily, "You can be disagreeable, cantankerous and rude if you like, but there's not that much difference between us, Zara. I may only be part volk, but you would not have known it had I not told you. I am not ashamed of who I am, but I think you should be. Surely a little decency cannot be so difficult to find."

Zara stopped in her tracks, feeling somewhat puzzled by his words. She returned to the fence where she stood with her head cocked slightly to one side.

"How did you know my name? I did not tell you."

"I… I don't know," Salvador stuttered, "I just knew."

For a moment, the two wolves stared at each other in silence. Then Zara nodded respectfully and walked away, leaving a confused, but happy Salvador. He returned to his cave, trying to make sense of what had just passed between them. His sister, Fayth, was well known for her heightened awareness, but this was the first time he had experienced it himself. He wondered if his gift would be like hers, but a full stomach and heavy contemplation had made him rather tired, and Salvador soon fell asleep.

In their mountain home, life for Salvador's former pack had slowly moved forward. His siblings played rougher than they had before, sharpening their skills and learning their place within a hunt. All except for Fayth, who spent her time watching how her mother ruled and guided the pack. She could see Akea was quietly preparing them for something, and she hoped as she had always done, that they would be ready. Fayth had taken Salvador's loss hard and she could not bear to lose anyone else.

In the cool air of the early evening, the pack came together for the howling. It gave everyone a sense of security and belonging, as well as serving to proclaim their strength and number to neighbouring packs. Fayth's howl was of a much higher pitch than her siblings, which gave it an eerie quality. Although it stood out if she howled alone, when she joined in with her family, it formed a perfect harmony.

"Stop!" cried Fayth. Everyone fell silent and stared at her. Even through the howling she had heard something. "Listen!" she said calmly, tilting her head to one side.

They all listened carefully and sure enough, a howl could be heard in the distance. Kazakh stood upright and tense, and as other howls joined the first, his alpha instincts erupted into a territorial bark.

"Enough!" snapped Akea, as she moved to stand beside her mate. "These volks are too far away to be a threat for now. They have heard the howling and will know we are here. Let that be enough for now. We do not want them to think us concerned by their presence."

Reluctantly, Kazakh agreed. They had known this moment would come. They had been preparing for it since Salvador's disappearance, but there was no need to hasten it. Much to their relief, the strange wolves made no appearance that night, but both Akea and Kazakh knew it was only a matter of time before things changed.

Chapter 6

The following weeks were glorious – well, at least Salvador thought so. He still had his artificial cave, his artificial rock and his artificial pool, but his new neighbour was very real indeed. Salvador studied her each day, observing the changes in her temperament and behaviour, learning to recognise when he could approach her enclosure and when to let her be. He missed the company of other wolves very much, but realised his friendship with Zara could not be rushed.

Salvador walked the perimeter of his enclosure each day, with a dedication his father would be proud of. It wasn't much in the way of territory, but it was his, and patrolling it helped him to feel connected to his family, even if it saddened him a little.

One morning, as he passed along the edge of Zara's enclosure, he was so deep in thought he didn't notice her trotting over.

"Good morning, Salvador," she called out cheerfully, her tail wagging gently from side to side in friendly greeting. For a moment, Salvador was stunned into silence. He couldn't believe she was being nice to him, and much sooner than he had expected too.

"Good... good morning, Zara," he stuttered in reply. His obvious surprise brought a smile to her face, which made her look quite pretty. She wasn't beautiful like Akea or Gwenevier, for her coat was rough and her face rather plain looking, but the smile had softened her features and made her seem friendlier. As Salvador looked into her eyes, he was sure they had just established a deeper understanding and he could be less cautious about approaching her in future.

The weeks seemed to pass with greater speed now Salvador had someone to talk to. Now he was more inclined to sleep outside during the day. That way, the last thing he would see before closing his eyes, was Zara. Her presence gave him comfort, and although she would not care to admit it, Zara felt the same way about Salvador.

Zara lay dozing by the fence, enjoying the warmth of the sun on her back, when the sound of whimpering disturbed her. It was coming from Salvador's pen. She could see him asleep beneath a tree, his legs paddling frantically. It seemed more of a nightmare than a pleasant dream. She was about to speak to him when she heard footsteps behind her and turned to see Max approaching. He gave a couple of short whistles and clicks before calling Zara by her park name.

"Dusky, come on girl, come on." The sound of his voice woke Salvador, who mistook his arrival for feeding time and started yipping excitedly and jumping about. He rushed down to the fence, but Max did not have the wheelbarrow with him, and a disappointed Salvador fell silent.

Max stood by the fence dividing the enclosures and grasped the rope that hung there with both hands. When he pulled hard on the rope, the loud clanking and squeaking that resulted spooked both animals, and they retreated to a safer distance. Zara was first to spot the appearance of a doorway between the enclosures and she approached it cautiously before slipping through into Salvador's pen. Max watched them closely, power hose at the ready, in case they needed separating again. Allowing the two animals together would put their friendship to the test, but if they hoped to develop a fully functioning pack, then establishing an alpha pair was a vital first step.

Salvador was so delighted to get up close to his friend at last that he seemed to forget his manners. He turned away from the fence and bounced onto Zara with great enthusiasm, knocking her to the ground.

"Get off!" she snapped angrily, pushing him away and shaking herself. She was not ready to celebrate the new arrangement just yet. Her prime concern was to investigate her new surroundings and determine who was in charge. Salvador watched indignantly as she nosed around inside 'his' cave, then around 'his' trees and rocks, and finally drank from 'his' pool. It took every ounce of the self-control he could muster to remain silent.

Zara glanced at him before squatting on the grass and walking away with her head and tail held high. Salvador sniffed the patch of grass where Zara had urinated. Its strong scent reinforced the confident behaviour she displayed from the moment she walked in. This healthy young female had just claimed 'his' enclosure as her own. Well, no matter what she did, this was still 'his' enclosure and he was going to prove it. He marched confidently over to 'his' tree and cocked a hind leg, leaving his own scent behind in a gesture of defiance. "Two can play at that game," he muttered to himself.

Zara watched him from beneath the shelter of another tree, the sun breaking through the leaves and dancing on her back. Salvador adopted a low stalking position, moving slowly towards her. Max stood there, hands firmly gripping the power hose just in case things turned nasty.

Salvador reached the tree without any reaction from Zara. Then she bolted out from under it and span round to face him, letting out a playful bark. Salvador lunged for her throat, but Zara was too quick for him. She landed a neat swipe across his muzzle and the pair tumbled to the ground in a tussle of teeth and paws. Max chuckled - as an experienced keeper he knew no matter how fierce this looked, they were only play fighting.

After a while, they stretched out on the grass and groomed one another. For the first time in months, Salvador felt truly content. He was part of a pack again, even if it was only a pack of two.

Smiling, Max put down the power hose and walked away. He could see there would be no need for it now. His departure reminded

Salvador that he and Zara had been 'put' together, and he didn't know why. He turned to Zara who lay on her side, lazily flicking her tail back and forth.

"I wonder why you and I were put together," he said with his head cocked to one side.

"I do not know," she replied. "Perhaps Max does not wish us to be lonely. After all, he is most thoughtful for a human. Or there may not even be a reason for it. I am sure it will become clearer in time."

Salvador knew he should be grateful for the company. Indeed, he was grateful, but he knew from experience that humans could not be trusted, and he couldn't help thinking that there was more to this situation than either of them could see.

Chapter 7

In the calm of the midday heat, Akea stood proudly on the alpha's rock, her blue eyes surveying both the land and the resting pack beneath her. Fayth lay a short distance behind, watching her intently, and taking in every movement of the head and subtle twitching of the ears. The wolf Queen was aware of the strange, unearthly feeling her daughter's gaze bestowed on others. At this moment, she could sense it was directed at her, without even needing to turn around.

"Why do you watch me, my daughter?" she asked calmly, turning towards her with a warm smile. Fayth tilted her head and thought for a moment. She was sure her mother knew the answer to that question better than she did herself.

"I can think of no reasonable explanation, my mother. I only know that I must watch you, and..." Fayth stopped abruptly and stood up, her fur bristling with agitation. She trotted to the edge of the alpha's rock, lowered her head and growled. Akea's fur bristled too, and as she loomed over Fayth's shoulder, feeling the same strange sensation, she was unable to stop herself from joining in her daughter's growl.

The unwelcome feeling disappeared as quickly as it had come, and had it not been for the sharing of it, Akea would have been able to dismiss it. But they had both experienced the same sensation of approaching danger, and it had felt much nearer than she would have liked. Akea gently nuzzled her daughter, and without saying a word she made her way down the rock in search of Kazakh, leaving Fayth to return to her look-out duties with as much composure as she could muster.

****

If it had been up to Max, Salvador and Zara would be allowed to mature, breed and expand the size of their pack as naturally as possible. Unfortunately, it wasn't up to him. Instead, it was his responsibility to oversee the gradual introduction of other wolves and try to make it as stress-free as possible.

In the beginning, things had gone well. Salvador had established himself as pack leader, and after a brief dispute with one of the females, Zara had claimed her place beside him.

The newest arrivals were three siblings, two silver-grey females, Hailie and Fantine, and their older brother, Rakin. He was a handsome grey wolf with a blue roan tinge to his fur and too great an opinion of himself for his own good.

Slipping through the opening into the larger enclosure, Hailie and Fantine were quick to acknowledge the alpha pair's rank by quietly submitting to a thorough inspection. They were just as quick to make friends with the other wolves, but Rakin's behaviour couldn't have been more different. He reluctantly submitted to the inspection before curling up, away from the others. He didn't seem to care if this older male was in charge or not. Salvador sensed he would be extremely troublesome, and he was right. Rakin was unresponsive to council or indeed, to anything.

One day, Salvador and Zara lay near the remains of a deer carcass, their pack spread out contentedly around them. Hailie and Fantine were nipping playfully at one another while the others, their stomachs full, could barely stay awake.

Rakin seized his chance and charged towards the carcass, hip-slamming Salvador aside. His ears were flat, his tail low and his back arched. This was a direct challenge to Salvador's authority. Filled with fury, Salvador lunged forward, viciously thrashing the young male and scattering the pack in surprise. They watched in a stunned silence at the unusual ferocity of a retaliation that only ended after Rakin's appeal for mercy.

Zara was concerned, but not surprised by it. She had seen the changes in Salvador in recent weeks. He had gradually become more like a wild wolf - a behavioural change that had not gone unnoticed by their keeper either. A suitably chastened Rakin slunk away to lick his wounds. Salvador had given him a beating he would not easily forget.

That night, as Salvador lay asleep in his cave, he began to dream: *Akea was there, standing at the edge of her territory with her entire pack behind her. Wolves he did not recognise came from beyond the horizon and attacked the pack. His family were clearly outnumbered. The opposing pack leader, a white wolf covered in scars, overwhelmed Akea and...*

"No!" cried Salvador, leaping out of the cave in a surging flood of terror. Zara rushed out to find Salvador curled tightly in a submissive posture, gasping for breath and unsure of his surroundings. He seemed afraid of everything that should have been familiar to him. She stood in front of her friend and licked him gently around the muzzle.

"What is it, my dear?" she whispered, "What is the matter?"

"I... I don't know," he replied hesitantly, still trying to get his bearings, "I have just had the strangest dream. It seemed so real."

"It was just a nightmare and you have had them before. Do not be concerned by it." Zara turned back towards the cave entrance, but Salvador did not follow.

"No, it was not," he insisted. The firmness of his reply surprised her, and she returned warily to his side.

"It was more than just a dream - it was real. I was watching a great battle between my family and a rival pack." Salvador paused for a moment, deep in thought. "Yes, I understand it now. It was a warning... a 'sub-shin-yair.'" Zara cocked her head to one side and gazed quizzically at him.

"A message?" she replied in disbelief, "It was only a dream, Salvador, and dreams can do strange things. They can seem real, but they are not messages." She turned again towards the cave entrance and Salvador reluctantly followed.

How could he expect Zara to understand? His family were descendants of the Great White Wolf, and when he had first arrived at the park, his mother had spoken to him. She had assured him the way forward would be revealed, and that the Great Wolf would be with him. Without doubt, this was a warning message, a 'sub-shin-yair'.

Chapter 8

Akea stirred, reluctantly woken from her blissful slumber by Kazakh. As she gazed sleepily about her, she could see it was barely light.

"Let me sleep, Kazakh," she muttered, resting her head back on her front paws, but Kazakh nudged her shoulder firmly with his muzzle.

"You must get up, my dear," he insisted, hurrying to the cave entrance. Akea opened her mouth wide in a yawning gape, arched her back and stood up. She could see Kazakh was extremely anxious.

"What's wrong?" she asked calmly.

"You must come with me at once. Your strange daughter has sensed our pack is being observed and the sentries have confirmed the appearance of an unknown pack on the horizon."

It usually amused her when Kazakh referred to them as 'her' children. They were always 'her' children when one of them displayed a behaviour Kazakh could not explain, and she knew exactly whose 'gift' of insight was worrying him now – Fayth's. She had sensed the presence of the other pack before, but this was the first time anyone had seen them, and it was a worrying development.

"I wish she had sensed the Great Volk instead," grumbled Kazakh as they hurried down to join the pack.

"I have asked him to be with our lost son for the remainder of his time away," replied Akea, "So it was unlikely to have been the Great Volk, anyway."

As they approached the anxious faces of their waiting pack, Kazakh slowed his pace and turned towards her.

"I hope he'll at least be watching over us too," he whispered anxiously.

"I am sure he will be," she replied, "For I believe nothing is beyond his capacity."

****

Like his family, Salvador was anxious too. His dreams continued to trouble him, clouding his mind even during the hours of daylight. Each time the images became more detailed.

Now he could clearly see the large alpha wolf attacking his mother. It was badly scarred, its coat long and white, and its right forelimb turned inward. It could not have risen so high in the ranks if this had been a birth defect. This was an animal crippled in the heat of battle.

As the light began to fade, Max arrived with the pack's meal. Salvador failed to notice. Suddenly, a voice rang out. "Salvador!" Startled, Salvador sat up. Then he saw the anxious gaze of his pack. Their eyes darted from the food to Salvador and back again. They were all hungry, but no one dared approach the food before him.

He hurried over to the carcass, hungrily tore off a chunk and returned to his place by the pool, to eat in peace. His strange behaviour was making Zara nervous. She'd never had to announce the arrival of a meal before. As she began to feed, the other wolves crept in warily to join her and the atmosphere gradually returned to normal.

The following evening, Salvador slept some distance away from the others. It was something he always did when he felt troubled and Zara thought it best not to interfere.

Again, the dream came to him, but this time stronger than ever before. Now, Salvador could even hear what was happening. This time, the rival wolf's attack grew in intensity, knocking Akea to the ground. As it moved in for the kill, Salvador dashed out into the rain, howling in despair.

"Are you mad?" snapped Zara, running to his side. "What is the meaning of this?" Salvador turned to face her, panting vigorously. His short, silky fur was already heavy with rain.

"I don't know how to explain this," he cried, "but I must leave the park. I must return to my mountain home before it is too late."

"This is nonsense, Salvador. You have had nightmares before and that is all this is. Come inside out of the rain."

"No!" barked Salvador. Zara took a step backwards. The force of his words was scaring her. She stared at him, her ears low and her tail tucked beneath her. Salvador could see her submissive behaviour but had to make her understand.

"These dreams are important. They are not the wanderings of my imagination and they are not just nightmares. My mother's life and the lives of my family are in danger. I must help them fight this unknown evil. If I stay here, my family will be lost, and I will be tormented forever." Even as his voice began to falter, he poured his heart into the last three words, "They need me."

"They need you?" she spluttered, "We need you, Salvador. We are your family now." A rumble of thunder rippled through the air, startling both animals, and as a second rumble erupted, Salvador spoke again, raising his voice to be heard over the storm.

"Come with me, Zara," he pleaded.

"I can't, Salvador. I've never been a wild wolf. This is the only home I have ever known.

"But you must, Zara - I cannot do this alone. Without a pack, I cannot hope to win this battle, and without you, there will always be a part of me missing. I love you Zara and I need you now more than I ever have before."

Feeling surprised and flattered, Zara looked away. In that moment, the clouds parted, and the moon shone down, bringing with it a sense of peace amid the chaos of the storm. A long, lonely howl echoed all around them and the figure of a lone white wolf appeared on the mountain peak. It was in that moment that Zara finally understood. The Great White Wolf was not just a legend, he was real. Akea had been chosen by him for a reason, and as his mother's son, so had Salvador.

"Oh Salvador," she said with a smile, "You know I love you and I will follow you to the ends of the earth if necessary. Let us save your Volk Queen together."

As they nuzzled and licked one another, the white wolf repeated his howl. This time, Salvador joined him, and the sound of howling filled the air, pushing the sound of thunder into the background. To Salvador, it felt as if Akea and all the wolves before her were with him now.

"Yes!" he barked in answer to them, "Tomorrow, I will go."

Chapter 9

The next morning, Max arrived to give the pack their breakfast. As his wheelbarrow rattled along the path, Salvador appeared at the entrance to the den. He had been awake well before dawn, working out his escape plan, and perhaps more importantly, how he would convince the rest of his pack to go with him. Just as Max reached the feeding hatch, Salvador trotted out to greet him with the other wolves close behind.

For his plan to succeed, it was vital this day appear just like any other - at least until Max was out of sight. So, without a word to the others, Salvador ate hungrily, nodding at Zara to do the same, and as the unsuspecting pack joined in, Max smiled and walked away.

"Eat as much as you can," ordered Salvador, as soon as Max was out of sight, "This will be the last meal we eat together here." Everyone stopped eating and stared at him, but it wasn't long before the mutterings of eleven puzzled faces replaced the brief silence.

"Do you remember the story of how I came to be here?" he asked.

"Of course, we do," muttered Rakin as the others fell silent again.

"I may have told you *how* I came to be here, Rakin, but I did not tell you *why*."

"We all have our stories, Salvador, but you don't see any of us making a mystery out of them." It would have given Salvador great satisfaction to put the young male in his place again, but now was not the time.

With as much confidence as he could muster, Salvador related the story of his mother's journey from husky pup to wolf Queen. It was a story that reminded Zara of her first meeting with Salvador and she shifted uncomfortably. She understood now he was far from the 'mongrel' she had called him then.

Salvador was a descendent of the Great White Wolf, a heritage that had not only allowed Akea to speak to him shortly after his arrival at the park, but one that had allowed the Great Wolf himself to guide Salvador through the visions she had been so determined to dismiss as nightmares. By the time Salvador had finished speaking, the others understood this too.

"Why do we have to go?" demanded Rakin, "We were not born into your pack. We are our own pack," he said proudly. "We should stay here."

"You may speak for yourself, brother," replied Hailie.

"But not for us," added Fantine, "How could we not follow the path the Great Wolf has so clearly laid out for us." It quickly became clear that the only wolf against leaving was Rakin. He seemed determined to find a worthy reason for them to stay and Salvador's patience was running out.

"Enough!" he snapped, fixing the youngster with an icy glare, "You may remain here if you wish, but the rest of us are leaving." Turning his back on Rakin, he returned to finish his meal, and the others soon followed him.

As the day progressed, Salvador discreetly outlined and repeated his plan for escape, pausing whenever Rakin was nearby. He doubted the young wolf's loyalty and as they would only have one chance to escape, the less Rakin knew, the greater the likelihood of their success.

When Max arrived with their evening meal, Salvador trotted over to greet him, his tail wagging gently in friendly greeting. Max smiled as he pushed open the door with the wheelbarrow and tossed him a small chunk of meat.

Seconds later, Max found himself pinned to the fence by Salvador with his hackles raised and a fierce growl erupting from his shaggy black frame. One by one, the pack made their way passed him and out through the open door.

Seeing the fear in the young man's eyes was hard for Salvador, for Max had always been kind to him, so as the last wolf left the enclosure, Salvador allowed his gaze to soften. Then he nodded respectfully, turned and trotted out after the others, leaving Max staring in disbelief as the pack disappeared into the distance.

Inside the wolf den, sat an equally unsettled Rakin. He liked his captive bred life and the feeling of security it gave him, but at the same time, he did not wish to be alone. His eyes darted from the open door to Max and back again, and he realised if he did not decide soon, it would be too late.

****

That night, the pack huddled together among the leaves collected at the side of a fallen tree. They had travelled a great distance, and exhaustion quickly overcame any anxiety raised by their first night beyond the familiar boundaries of the park. Rakin was still absent, and by now, it seemed unlikely he would be joining them.

Salvador lay at the edge of his sleeping pack, gazing dreamily up at the star-studded sky. Something about them reminded him of his mother and he wondered if she was gazing up at the same stars and thinking of him.

"Oh, Mother," he whispered, "I am coming to help you. I only wish there were some way for you to know this." Then, Salvador remembered that Akea had asked the Great White Wolf to watch over him and he felt compelled to return the favour. He closed his eyes for a moment before reaching out with his whole heart.

"Oh, Great One. I know it is by my mother's request you have been with me all this time, but now it is I who must ask you to watch over her. See that her pack is prepared for the battle to come. Please, help her understand that help is on its way. I thank you for guiding me, but now I am free,

I am ready. Please, see that my mother is also."

As Salvador opened his eyes, he saw a familiar figure, bathed in moonlight, watching from a distant hilltop. It howled softly before disappearing into the darkness. Filled with a strange inner peace, Salvador curled himself into a tight ball and fell asleep. The vision came to him again, but he was no longer afraid, for the Great White Wolf was with him.

Chapter 10

It was barely light when Salvador and Zara led their pack through the dense forest and rocky mountains that lay in their path. They stopped at regular intervals, allowing Salvador to carefully scan the area. He had been away long enough for the trails to seem unfamiliar, yet every fibre of his being assured him they were following the right path. Then, as they approached the next ridge, Salvador stopped and turned around.

"Come quickly, all of you," he cried out. Zara rushed to stand at her friend's side and the other wolves gathered around.

"Is this it?" she whispered excitedly, looking out at the picturesque landscape. Spread out before them lay the view Salvador had been waiting for, but as she followed his gaze, Zara realised he was not looking at the scene immediately below them, but at the caves in the distance. A gust of wind brought a familiar scent to Salvador's nose, and he howled triumphantly at the thought of what they had accomplished; home was just a day's travel away.

****

The rival pack drew closer with each passing day and it was only a matter of time before things came to a head. Kazakh was creeping nervously around the caves as if danger could leap out on him at any moment. Akea tried hard not to pay attention to it. She was training her pack harder each day, knowing their battle skills must be perfect if they were to have a chance of winning. There simply wasn't time to worry about Kazakh right now.

Only one member of Akea's pack knew of Salvador's approach. Fayth closed her eyes, blocking out the sounds around her and focusing her thoughts. "At last," she whispered to herself, "the Great Volk has shown his support for those who believe in him. My estranged brother returns to where he belongs. And he is not alone."

Opening her eyes, Fayth looked about her and smiled. Their chance of victory was now stronger than ever. She wanted to inform Akea, but she knew her brother would not arrive before the appointed time and it would be unkind to distract her mother right now, even with such wonderful news. Barely able to contain her excitement, Fayth looked around for the one wolf she knew could be trusted with such a secret.

As the only pack member with knowledge of hunting, Salvador had been providing his friends with the occasional small meal. If they were to be at full strength for the battle ahead, they would need to work together to take down something bigger.

He could remember following his mother's pack on hunting trips. The memories were as clear as if engraved within the walls of his mind. He searched the woodland as they made their way carefully through it, hoping to catch a glimpse of something suitable. As they approached a fallen tree, Salvador stopped abruptly. He dropped to the ground and the others quickly followed his lead.

"What is it?" asked Zara, creeping forward to join him. Salvador jerked his head towards the clearing ahead of them, and following his gaze, Zara caught sight of a large deer picking out grass shoots from among the thicket.

The sable coloured she-wolf lowered her head, her eyes narrowing as she did so. Although a captive bred wolf, her predatory instincts stirred deep within her, and as she licked her lips, her silky tail stopped swaying, and stiffened.

The other wolves sensed the change in her and moved forward, eager to catch a glimpse of the prey. Salvador closed his eyes for a moment, focusing his thoughts on the wolves behind him before turning to Zara and nodding. Lifting each paw carefully off the ground, they stalked the deer. The rest of the pack fanned out, slowly encircling their unsuspecting prey.

They had not gone far when the deer looked up from the bracken, its nostrils twitching warily. Salvador stopped dead in his tracks. The creature's anxiety puzzled him. They were stalking it from downwind; it couldn't possibly have detected them yet.

The deer barked in alarm and took flight as a lean, grey figure broke cover and began racing towards it. For a moment, the wolf pack stared at each other in surprise before setting off in pursuit. They soon found the deer lying motionless on the ground, with the lone wolf standing confidently over it.

"Well, I hope you have brought your own food, for there is barely enough here for a party," he sniggered, looking at their puzzled faces.

"Javier!" cried Salvador in disbelief. "Is it really you? What are you doing here?" The two wolves licked each other enthusiastically around the muzzle while the others looked on.

"Of course, it's me," laughed Javier, "Fayth sent me to meet you; she sensed your approach."

"And my mother and father?"

"They are well, my friend," replied Javier gently, "but they do not know you are here. Fayth thought it best not to distract them."

Salvador stood quietly for a moment, lost in his thoughts. He knew Fayth had made the right choice, but he couldn't help a twinge of disappointment that Javier had not been sent by his mother.

A gentle nudge at his shoulder reminded him that Zara and the others had been waiting patiently. He turned to see her smiling at him and rubbed his muzzle affectionately against hers before introducing his friends to Javier.

They approached him nervously, but he lowered his head and ears, politely submitting to their curiosity. With the introductions over, Javier stepped aside, and Salvador and his friends ate hungrily.

Suddenly, a howl echoed all around them and they looked up in alarm. Salvador's heart thumped heavily against his chest. Only he and Javier understood the meaning of this sound - a wolf's battle cry.

Chapter 11

An eagle shrieked as it circled over the gathering wolves below. On one side of the valley, Akea's pack stood erect; ready to support their Queen and defend their land. The rival pack had gathered on the opposite side, led by a white she-wolf. They vastly outnumbered Akea's pack, and she knew it.

Akea closed her eyes, reaching out once more to the Great White Wolf and placing her life in his care. Then, taking in a long, deep breath, she tilted her head high and howled. With the sound filling the valley, the two wolf packs came thundering towards each other.

The air filled with the sounds of snarling and snapping as the animals came together in battle. Fayth lunged forward, grabbing her opponent by the neck and sending the pair of them tumbling. Akea and Kazakh fought their way towards the opposing alpha pair. Their only hope of winning such an uneven battle would be to defeat its leaders as swiftly as possible, but coming face to face with her scarred enemy, Akea halted.

"Bluinse!" she barked, surprised to see Kazakh's sister standing there, "It can't be you. I saw you fall to your death."

"How do you think I got this?" snapped Bluinse, raising a crippled paw in reply. The other wolves heard the verbal exchange and stopped fighting, curious to find out how the two females knew each other.

"This is turning into quite the family reunion," laughed Bluinse, turning to her companion. Kazakh followed her gaze, his hackles rising as he saw his brother.

"Maska!" he snarled angrily, "I might have known. I should not have been so lenient when we quarreled." Maska snorted but said nothing - clearly Bluinse was the dominant partner here.

"Well, your majesty," she began, "you have made yourself at home." What started as a mocking tone, now became more menacing. "But now, I am here to take what is mine."

"How dare you!" cried Fayth, stamping her paw in defiance, "How dare you come here and lay claim to something that was never yours to begin with."

"You are certainly your mother's child, but I fear someone has misled you, my dear. Before your husky mother was even born, I was considered successor to the old Volk Queen. Your mother stole my position, and she took Kazakh away from his family, so that she could control the pack."

Kazakh snarled in a mixture of defiance and disbelief. He remembered clearly the first time he set eyes on Akea; how he had sensed something great in her. He recalled with pride the courage she had shown in biting him when he attacked her father, and he remembered all they had been through since then.

"You speak nothing but lies, my sister," he cried, "The Volk Queen herself acknowledged Akea as the successor chosen by the Great Volk - but enough of this. There is only one way to end this argument."

With that, Kazakh launched himself at Bluinse, signalling a fresh start to the fighting. Moments later, a chorus of howls filled the air, and everyone looked up to find yet another pack of wolves charging down the hill towards them.

Akea was overjoyed to see they were led by Salvador. Her faith in the Great Wolf had been rewarded. Bluinse turned and headed straight for him. There could be no greater blow to Akea than to kill her son, and she would be more than a match for this inexperienced youth.

Salvador's pack joined with Akea's, and seeing the tide of battle turning against them, many of Bluinse's pack fled into the forest. Javier and Adair led a group of wolves in pursuit, while the rest fought those foolish enough to remain behind.

Rising on their hind legs, Salvador and Bluinse threw themselves together, biting savagely and tumbling to the ground. Bluinse was older and wiser, but her crippled paw was proving a hindrance. With a well-timed swipe, Salvador knocked her injured limb out from under her, and as she lost her balance, he used his bodyweight to knock her down and pin her to the floor. Maska tried to come to her aid, but found his path blocked by both Kazakh and Akea.

"It's over, Bluinse!" Salvador called loudly, "No one trifles with my family." Bluinse's body relaxed beneath his weight, announcing her defeat.

"You are not just your mother's son," she acknowledged, "You have the Great Volk within you." Salvador took a step back and allowed his aunt to get up.

"Leave this place," he demanded, "and if you ever set foot on our land again, I will kill you." With the threat of death hanging over her, Bluinse howled to the remaining members of her pack, and together with Maska, they disappeared into the distance.

It was well after midnight before Salvador finally had a moment to himself. It had been an emotional reunion with his parents, not to mention all the explanations and introductions that had been needed. He was sitting on the edge of the alpha's rock, taking in deep calming breaths, when Fayth came to sit beside him.

"Why did you let Bluinse go?" she asked softly.

"I don't know," he answered, "for some reason, it seemed the right thing to do." Fayth said nothing. Her brother may have answered her question, but she could see there was something far more important on his mind. They sat in silence for a short while before Salvador spoke again.

"While I was away, I began experiencing strange dreams, dreams about the recent battle. They were so vivid, and they felt so real. I was convinced they were warning messages, messages telling me that I needed to be here." Fayth's eyes beamed up at him, full of love and reassurance.

"My dear brother, I see I am not the only one to possess a gift. You have the ability to deliver warning messages through your dreams, just as I can sense things that others cannot."

"I felt the presence of the Legendary Great White Volk too," he added. "Indeed, I believe I even saw him. Do you believe in him, Fayth?"

"I believe he exists," she replied, "but that he only appears to those who truly need him. I have not seen him, but I sense he is no ordinary volk; his markings are strange, he lives for countless years, and he is the wisest of all our kind."

They both looked up as a shooting star rushed across the sky. It was a beautiful night, but one thing lay heavily on Salvador's mind, preventing him from truly appreciating it.

"Fayth, what does the future hold for us?" he asked, and Fayth smiled thoughtfully.

"I believe the world is far from done with us. There will be challenges, some of which will trouble us greatly, but we need not be afraid of what lies ahead, my brother. We have our gifts, you and I, and our family. And most importantly, we have the Great White Volk to guide us always, for he lives within us all."

Thank you for reading
Akea – His Mother's Son.

If you enjoyed it, I hope you will tell
your friends or leave a brief review
on Amazon or Goodreads.

Be sure to subscribe to my newsletter or blog
at www.elizabethjade.org and be among the
first to know when a new title is available.

Thanks again for reading
Akea – His Mother's Son.

Best Wishes
Elizabeth Jade